THE BLOOMSBURY B[...]

Mother and Daughter Poems

For Dot and Lucy,
with much love

THE BLOOMSBURY BOOK OF

Mother and Daughter Poems

SELECTED BY
FIONA WATERS

ILLUSTRATED BY
CHRISTOPHER CORR

BLOOMSBURY

First published in Great Britain in 2000
Bloomsbury Publishing Plc, 38 Soho Square, London, W1V 5DF

Individual poem details feature on the acknowledgements page situated at the back of this book
Copyright © Text this selection Fiona Waters 2000
Copyright © Illustrations Christopher Corr 2000

The moral right of the author has been asserted
A CIP catalogue record of this book is available from the
British Library

ISBN 0 7475 4745 9

Printed in England by St Edmundsbury Press

10 9 8 7 6 5 4 3 2 1

Contents

The Daisy Field	9
Lemon Sole	10
Woman Enough	12
At an Audition	15
Rebecca, Sweet-one, Little-one	16
The Flowers	18
Golden Bangles: for My Indian Daughter	20
Folding Sheets	22
My Mother	23
Eat Your Veg	24
Fanfare	26
What Your Mother Tells You Now	29
The Moment	30
Small Incident in Library	32
Morning Song	34
Mama	36

Lullaby   38
Poem for a Daughter   40
Accomplishments   42
Young   44
Annie (1868-1944)   46
Names   48
Sweet Song for Katie   50
A Frosty Night   52
Doorsteps   54
Gift for Rebecca   56
Sleep, Darling   58
Do Not Despise Me   59
Dressed to Spill   60
On Platform 5   62
When I was a Child   64
Two Mangy Cooks   66
Soup   67
To Our Daughter   68
Clinic Day   70
Mother . . . Sister . . . Daughter   72
Mothers and Daughters   73

The Glassy Green and Maroon	74
Yesterday	76
For My Grandmother Knitting	78
Motherless Baby	81
Human Affection	81
Broken Moon (for Emma)	82
The Dolls	84
Uniform	85
Whose Baby?	86
Science, 1953	88
Praise Song for My Mother	90
Two Old Women	91
It's Mother, You See	92
Tell Me, Tell Me, Sarah Jane	94

The Daisy Field

The telephone breaks through my sleep.
'Is that you darling? Mummy here.'
A girl's voice still
in this her ninetieth year.

Warm grass and cuckoo-sharpened air,
the buttercup glowed gold beneath her chin.
Five-year-old fingers worked
green, yellow, white, encircled hair
and limbs with gentle chains.
Four decades on, they still hang there,
'Is that you, darling? Mummy here.'

Angela Kirby

Lemon Sole

I lay and heard voices
spin through the house
and there were five minutes to run
for the snow-slewed school bus.

My mother said they had caught it
as she wiped stars from the window –
the frost mended its web
and she put her snow-cool hand to my forehead.

The baby peeked round her skirts
trying to make me laugh
but I said my head hurt
and shut my eyes on her and coughed.

My mother kneeled
until her shape hid the whole world.
She buffed up my pillows as she held me.
'Could you eat a lemon sole?' she asked me.

It was her favourite
she would buy it as a treat for us.
I only liked the sound of it
slim, holy and expensive

but I said 'Yes, I will eat it'
and I shut my eyes and sailed out
on the noise of sunlight, white sheets
and lemon sole softly being cut up.

Helen Dunmore

Woman Enough

Because my grandmother's hours
were apple cakes baking,
& dust motes gathering
& linens yellowing
& seams and hems
inevitably unravelling –
I almost never keep house –
though really I *like* houses
& wish I had a clean one.

Because my mother's minutes
were sucked into the roar
of the vacuum cleaner,
because she waltzed with the washer-dryer
& tore her hair waiting for repairmen –
I send out my laundry,
& live in a dusty house,
though I really *like* clean houses
as well as anyone.

I am woman enough
to love the kneading of bread
as much as the feel
of typewriter keys
under my fingers –
springy, springy.
& the smell of clean laundry
& simmering soup
are almost as dear to me
as the smell of paper and ink.

I wish there were not a choice;
I wish I could be two women.
I wish the days could be longer.
But they are short.
So I write while
the dust piles up.

I sit at my typewriter
remembering my grandmother
& all my mothers,
& the minutes they lost
loving houses better than themselves –
& the man I love cleans up the kitchen

grumbling only a little
because he knows
that after all these centuries
it is easier for him
than for me.

Erica Jong

At an Audition

'Remember to smile darling,'
someone whispers, and there's a flurry
of hairbrushes – as if just one more polish
would make all the difference.
Then the children are gone:
scampering off white-socked like lambs.

It is the mothers who are nervous.
Left on their own they glance at magazines,
light cigarettes, or huddle together
against a wind that tells them
one day soon their darlings
will either disappoint or move beyond them.

Vicki Feaver

Rebecca, Sweet-one, Little-one

Rebecca, sweet-one, little-one
Siobhain Levy, fur-pie, loveliness,
sweet-face, sleepy head, Becca,
Becalla, lovely-one, loved-one,
sweet-pie, my favorite, my dear
one, nudnik, silly-face, sweetness,
dear-heart, little terror, little
madness, how many messages you
draw for me,
I love you Mommy
Becky, love, love, Becky, Love
I hate you Mommy
dark eyes
dark eyes
all those secrets you
give me
(Don't tell my teacher, they
write it on a form, they
put it in a file for
hundreds to read.)
and I

16

hot repository of
all your moods
have birthed you
quick and
shocking creature
you run
like a needle
through my life.

Susan Griffin

The Flowers

After lunch my daughter picked
handfuls of the wild flowers
she knew her grandfather liked best
and piled them in the basket of her bicycle,
beside an empty jam-jar and a trowel;
then, swaying like a candle-bearer,
she rode off to the church
and, like a little dog, I followed her.

She cleared the grave of nettles
and wild parsley, and dug a shallow hole
to put the jam-jar in. She arranged
the flowers to look their best
and scraped the moss from the stone,
so you could see whose grave
she had been caring for.
It didn't take her long – no longer
than making his bed in the morning
when he had got too old to help her.

Not knowing how to leave him,
how to say good-bye, I hesitated
by the rounded grave. *Come on*,
my daughter said, *It's finished now.*
And so we got our bicycles and rode home
down the lane, moving apart
and coming together again,
in and out of the ruts.

Selima Hill

19

Golden Bangles: for My Indian Daughter

It is twelve years since I first put on
these bangles. Circles
of yellow Indian gold,
they bruised the bones of my hand
as I pulled them on.
I sleep in them: my husband
can tell my mood
from the sound of my bangles
in the dark.

No ornaments, they are
like hair or fingernails part
of my body.
One has a raised design
or spell. The other
is plain, and dented
by my children's teeth.

Daughter, on your wedding day
I will put gold bangles
on your wrists. Gold
to protect you from want
in strangers' houses, and
for beauty: lying down naked
as on the night you were born,
you shall wear upon your dark skin
gold from this distant country
of your birth.

Erica Mumford

Folding Sheets

They must be clean.
There ought to be two of you
to talk as you work, your
eyes and hands meeting.
They can be crisp, a little rough
and fragrant from the line;
or hot from the dryer
as from the oven. A silver
grey kitten with amber
eyes to dart among
the sheets and wrestle and leap out
helps. But mostly pleasure
lies in the clean linen
slapping into shape.
Whenever I fold a fitted sheet
making moves that are like
closing doors, I feel my mother.
The smell of clean laundry is hers.

Marge Piercy

My Mother

My mother's smell is sweet or sour and moist
like the soft red cover of the apple.
She sits among her boxes, lace and tins
And notices the smallest of all breezes,
As if she were a tree upon the mountain
Growing away with no problem at all.

Her swan's head quivers like a light-bulb:
Does she breed in perfect peace, a light sleep,
Or smothered like a clock whose alarm
Is unendurable, whose featureless
Straight face is never wrong?
No-one knows what goes on inside a clock.

Medbh McGuckian

Eat Your Veg

Go on, try the artichoke,
Yes I agree they look
A bit unappetising,
But that TV cook

That you like, gave us the recipe,
And it doesn't taste too bad,
Well how about the peas then?
They're the best *I've* ever had.

What do you mean onions and peppers,
Are too crunchy when you chew?
That's the lamest excuse ever,
Just try a piece ... won't you?

These tomatoes are full of vitamins,
Oh yes, you hate the seeds,
Will you taste the aubergine?
Then how about some swedes?

Daddy's done these parsnips specially,
Would you like a wedge?
Oh, come on, don't be difficult,
Mummy, eat your veg.

Valerie Bloom

Fanfare

(for Winifrid Fanthorpe, born 5 February 1895, died
13 November 1978)

*Y*ou, in the old photographs, are always
The one with the melancholy half–smile, the one
Who couldn't quite relax into the joke.

My extrovert dog of a father,
With his ragtime blazer and his swimming togs
Tucked like a swiss roll under his arm,
Strides in his youth towards us down some esplanade,

Happy as Larry. You, on his other arm,
Are anxious about the weather forecast,
His overdraft, or early closing day.

You were good at predicting failure: marriages
Turned out wrong because you said they would.
You knew the rotations of armistice and war,
Watched politicians' fates with gloomy approval.

All your life you lived in a minefield,
And were pleased in a quiet way, when mines
Exploded. You never actually said
I told you so, but we could tell you meant it.

Crisis was your element. You kept your funny stories,
Your music-hall songs for doodlebug and blitz-nights.
In the next cubicle, after a car-crash, I heard you
Amusing the nurses with your trench wit through the blood.

Magic alerted you. Green, knives and ladders
Will always scare me through your tabus.
Your nightmare was Christmas; so much organized
Compulsory whoopee to be got through.

You always had some stratagem for making
Happiness keep its distance. Disaster
Was what you planned for. You always
Had hoarded loaves or candles up your sleeve.

Houses crumbled about your ears, taps leaked,
Electric light bulbs went out all over England,
Because for you homes were only provisional,
Bivouacs on the stony mountain of living.

You were best at friendship with chars, gipsies,
Or very far-off foreigners. Well-meaning neighbours
Were dangerous because they lived near.

Me too you managed best at a distance. On the landline
From your dugout to mine, your nightly
Pass, friend was really often quite jovial.

You were the lonely figure in the doorway
Waving goodbye in the cold, going back to a sink-full
Of crockery dirtied by those you loved. We
Left you behind to deal with our crusts and gristle.

I know why you chose now to die. You foresaw
Us approaching the Delectable Mountains,
And didn't feel up to all the cheers and mafficking.

But how, dearest, will even you retain your
Special brand of hard-bitten stoicism
Among the halleluyas of the triumphant dead?

UA Fanthorpe

What Your Mother Tells You Now

What your mother tells you now
in time
you will come to know.

Mitsuye Yamada

The Moment

When I saw the dark Egyptian stain,
I went down into the house to find you, Mother —
past the grandfather clock, with its huge
ochre moon, past the burnt
sienna woodwork, rubbed and glazed.
I went deeper and deeper down into the
body of the house, down below the
level of the earth. It must have been
the maid's day off, for I found you there
where I had never found you, by the wash tubs,
your hands thrust deep in soapy water,
and above your head, the blazing windows
at the surface of the ground.

You looked up from the iron sink,
a small haggard pretty woman
of 40, one week divorced.
'I've got my period, Mom,' I said,
and saw your face abruptly break open and
glow with joy. 'Baby,' you said,
coming toward me, hands out and
covered with tiny delicate bubbles like seeds.

Sharon Olds

Small Incident in Library

The little girl is lost among the books.
Two years old maybe, in bobble cap,
White lacy tights, red coat. She stands and looks.
'Can't see you, Mummy.' Mummy, next row up,
Intent on reading answers absently:
'I'm here, love.' Child calls out again: 'Can't see.'

A large man, his intentions of the best,
Stoops: 'Where's Mummy, then?' Child backs away.
Now the tall shelves threaten like a forest.
She toddles fast between them, starts to cry,
Takes the next aisle down and as her mother
Rounds one end disappears behind the other.

I catch the woman's tired-eyed prettiness.
We smile, shake heads. The child comes back in sight,
Hurtles to her laughing, hugs her knees:
'Found you!', in such ringing pure delight
It fills the room, there's no one left who's reading.
The mother looks down, blinking. 'Great soft thing.'

David Sutton

Morning Song

Love set you going like a fat gold watch.
The midwife slapped your footsoles, and your bald cry
Took its place among the elements.

Our voices echo, magnifying your arrival. New statue.
In a draughty museum, your nakedness
Shadows our safety. We stand round blankly as walls.

I'm no more your mother
Than the cloud that distils a mirror to reflect its own slow
Effacement at the wind's hand.

All night your moth-breath
Flickers among the flat pink roses. I wake to listen:
A far sea moves in my ear.

One cry, and I stumble from bed, cow-heavy and floral
In my Victorian nightgown.
Your mouth opens clean as a cat's. The window square

Whitens and swallows its dull stars. And now you try
Your handful of notes;
The clear vowels rise like balloons.

Sylvia Plath

Mama

She was a basketball player
In the Oklahoma Panhandle, 1916.
Dark-eyed, innocently graceful
In serge bloomers and middy blouse.
Her black-stockinged legs seemed to go on forever
Running, jumping: and – she could shoot!
Dead-eye, every time.
Even at seventy-five, heaped on her reclining chair,
Half blind and mad as hell,
She managed to sail across the kitchen a cast iron skillet
That nearly decapitated Dad.
He probably never moved so fast in his life –
Certainly not the night my sister was born
To Mama alone in bed in the three-room Boston apartment.
'Oh, you poor thing,' said the geology Ph.D.
And part-time piano tuner, looking for his hat
Before he even started to get the car,
Which was parked six blocks away –
By the time he got back
Mama had her new, unwashed baby,
And she never forgave him for that – or anything else;

Settled into a lifetime of nagging and eating.
Last time I saw that flesh was piled on a hospital morgue table,
But it wasn't Mama, though it wore her old size-40 bathrobe
and felt slippers.
No, it was an Oklahoma grasshopper's outgrown shell
That had to be dropped off somewhere,
So Mama could go back to playing basketball
Out in the great New West
Where Oklahoma goes on forever –
Where in pure joy she jumps to intercept somebody's ball,
Turns, ducks out of reach, bounces it once
And, with that solemn, sure child's gaze,
Takes dead-aim to shoot –
And score the winning basket of the game!

Janet Adkins

Lullaby

Go to sleep, Mum,
I won't stop breathing
suddenly, in the night.

Go to sleep, I won't
climb out of my cot and
tumble downstairs.

Mum, I won't swallow
the pills the doctor gave you or
put hairpins in electric
sockets, just go to sleep.

I won't cry
when you take me to school and leave me:
I'll be happy with other children
my own age.

Sleep, Mum, sleep.
I won't
fall in the pond, play with matches,
run under a lorry or even consider
sweets from strangers.

No, I won't
give you a lot of lip,
not like some.

I won't sniff glue,
fail all my exams,
get myself/
my girlfriend pregnant.
I'll work hard and get a steady/
really worthwhile job.
I promise, go to sleep.

I'll never forget
to drop in/phone/write
and if
I need any milk, I'll yell.

Rosemary Norman

Poem for a Daughter

'I think I'm going to have it,'
I said, joking between pains.
The midwife rolled competent
sleeves over corpulent milky arms.
'Dear, you never have it,
we deliver it.'
A judgement years proved true.
Certainly I've never had you

as you still have me, Caroline.
Why does a mother need a daughter?
Heart's needle, hostage to fortune,
freedom's end. Yet nothing's more perfect
than that bleating, razor-shaped cry
that delivers a mother to her baby.
The bloodcord snaps that held
their sphere together. The child,
tiny and alone, creates the mother.

A woman's life is her own
until it is taken away
by a first particular cry.
Then she is not alone
but part of the premises
of everything there is:
a time, a tribe, a war.
When we belong to the world
we become what we are.

Anne Stevenson

Accomplishments

I painted a picture – green sky – and showed it to my mother.
She said that's nice, I guess.
So I painted another holding the paintbrush in my teeth,
Look, Ma, no hands. And she said
I guess someone would admire that if they knew
How you did it and they were interested in painting
    which I am not.

I played clarinet solo in Gounod's Clarinet Concerto
With the Buffalo Philharmonic. Mother came to listen and said
That's nice, I guess.
So I played it with the Boston Symphony,
Lying on my back and using my toes,
Look, Ma, no hands. And she said
I guess someone would admire that if they knew
How you did it and they were interested in music
    which I am not.

I made an almond soufflé and served it to my mother.
She said that's nice, I guess.
So I made another, beating it with my breath,
Serving it with my elbows,
Look, Ma, no hands. And she said
I guess someone would admire that if they knew
How you did it and they were interested in eating
    which I am not.

So I sterilized my wrists, performed the amputation, threw away
My hands and went to my mother, but before I could say
Look, Ma, no hands, she said
I have a present for you and insisted I try on
The blue kid-gloves to make sure they were the right size.

Cynthia MacDonald

43

Young

A thousand doors ago
when I was a lonely kid
in a big house with four
garages and it was summer
as long as I could remember,
I lay on the lawn at night
clover wrinkling under me,
my mother's window a funnel
of yellow heat running out,
my father's window, half shut,
an eye where sleepers pass,
and the boards of the house
were smooth and white as wax
and probably a million leaves
sailed on their strange stalks
as the crickets ticked together,
and I, in my brand new body,
which was not a woman's yet,
told the stars my questions

and thought God could really see
the heat and the painted light,
elbows, knees, dreams, goodnight.

Anne Sexton

Annie *(1868-1944)*

I called her Ga, and a child's stuttered
syllable became her name.
A widow nearly forty years,
beautiful and straight-backed,
always with a bit of lace about her,
pearls the colour of her twisted hair,
the scent of lavender.

It was our job at Fforest to feed the hens
with cool and liquid handfuls of thrown corn.
We looked for eggs smuggled in hedge and hay,
and walked together the narrow path to the sea
calling the seals by their secret names.

At Christmas she rustled packages under her bed
where the po was kept and dusty suitcases.
That year I got an old doll with a china face,
ink-dark eyes and joints at elbows and knees.
Inside her skull, like a tea-pot, under her hair,
beneath her fontanelle, was the cold cave
where her eye-wires rocked her to sleep.

Somewhere in a high hospital window –
I drive past it sometimes with a start of loss –
her pale face made an oval in the glass
over a blue dressing-gown. She waved to me,
too far away to be certain it was her.
They wouldn't let children in.
Then she was lost or somebody gave her away.

Gillian Clarke

Names

She was Eliza for a few weeks
When she was a baby –
Eliza Lily. Soon it changed to Lil.

Later she was Miss Steward in the baker's shop
And then 'my love', 'my darling', Mother.

Widowed at thirty, she went back to work
As Mrs Hand. Her daughter grew up,
Married and gave birth.

Now she was Nanna. 'Everybody
Calls me Nanna,' she would say to visitors.
And so they did – friends, tradesmen, the doctor.

In the geriatric ward
They used the patients' Christian names.
'Lil,' we said, 'or Nanna,'
But it wasn't in her file
And for those last bewildered weeks
She was Eliza once again.

Wendy Cope

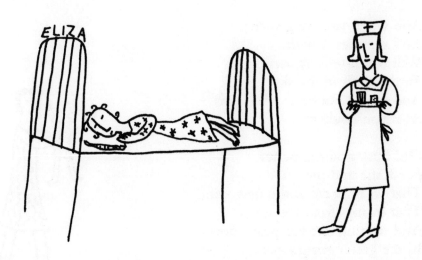

Sweet Song for Katie

The white doves are cooing,
Oh! Katie my dear,
In the sun in the morning,
In the spring of the year.
The peace doves are cooing,
Oh! Kate can you hear?

And when you are grown
And summer is high,
Will you listen my darling
To the birds in the sky,
And spread out your wild arms
As if you could fly?

Oh! I ask nothing better
For Katie and me
That we're brave as the new wind
That springs from the sea,
And we sing like the peace doves
In the green mango tree.

For we'll build a new world,
When the cane grass is high,
And peace will drop softly
Like wings from the sky,
And the children will run,
And the wild birds will fly.

And all that I ask now
For Katie and me,
Is a faith that is strong
As the wind off the sea,
Blowing so loud
In the green mango tree,
With a song that is ceaseless
As a dove in a tree.

Dorothy Hewett

A Frosty Night

'Alice, dear, what ails you,
    Dazed and lost and shaken?
Has the chill night numbed you?
    Is it fright you have taken?'

'Mother, I am very well,
    I was never better.
Mother, do not hold me so,
    Let me write my letter.'

'Sweet, my dear, what ails you?'
    'No, but I am well.
The night was cold and frosty –
    There's no more to tell.'

'Ay, the night was frosty,
    Coldly gaped the moon,
Yet the birds seemed twittering
    Through green boughs of June.

'Soft and thick the snow lay,
     Stars danced in the sky –
Not all the lambs of May-day
     Skip so bold and high.

'Your feet were dancing, Alice,
     Seemed to dance on air,
You looked a ghost or angel
     In the star-light there.

'Your eyes were frosted star-light;
     Your heart, fire and snow.
Who was it said, 'I love you?'
     'Mother, let me go!'

Robert Graves

Doorsteps

*C*utting bread brings her hands back to me –
the left, with its thick wedding ring,
steadying the loaf. Small plump hands
before age shirred and speckled them.

She would slice not downwards but across
with an unserrated ivory-handled carving knife
bought from a shop in the Edgware Road,
an Aladdin's cave of cast-offs from good houses –
earls and countesses were hinted at.

She used to pare to an elegant thinness.
First she smoothed already-softened butter
on the upturned face of the loaf. Always white,
Coburg shape. Finely rimmed with crust the soft
halfmoon half-slices came to the tea table
herringboned across a doylied plate.

I saw away at stoneground wholemeal.
Each slice falling forward into the crumbs
to be spread with butter's counterfeit
is as thick as three of hers. Doorsteps
she'd have called them. And those were white
in our street, rubbed with hearthstone
so that they glared in the sun
like new-dried tennis shoes.

Pamela Gillilan

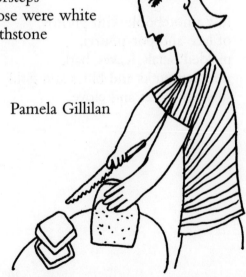

Gift for Rebecca

Not a Cinderella's castle,
nor a Barbie
with her chandelier clothes,
not silver-satin ribbons,
not a Polly-Pocket village,
nor Furby or toy lemur,
you've got those.

Just a notebook with photos
of lace and pot-pourri,
pickled petals, leaves, bark,
mingled pinks and blues and gold,
snips of violet and clove.

Here are pages that can hold you,
(not your legs, arms, toes),
the child
you make yourself from words,
the Rebecca of the strawberries,
the park, the school, the home,
the puzzles and surprises,
your very special treasures,
your head with its own rainbows
no one knows.

Mix your ginger and your glitter,
your vinegars and velvets,
loves, hates, thoughts, wishes;
catch a snowman as he goes.

Isobel Thrilling

Sleep, Darling

I have a small
daughter called
Cleis, who is
like a golden
flower

I wouldn't
take all Croesus'
kingdom with love
thrown in, for her

Sappho
(translated Mary Barnard)

Do Not Despise Me

Please do not despise me if I am
too old in the head and shoulders
too inadequately schooled
in the ins and outs of today
but since I've lived three score years
and am not high or low
wise or wealthy, I would
be grateful if I'm just accepted
as your other grandmother
who cannot speak English

Konai Helu Thaman

Dressed to Spill

A few tips for the first-time mum,
There's great joy, heaven knows,
But some adjustments must be made
When it comes to clothes.

Though once you were quite elegant
Dressed with care and style,
Believe me, standards start to plunge
And stay there for some while.

It's goodbye to those power suits,
It's breast not shoulder pad,
And your vital accessory?
A well-stocked changing bag!

It's also time to say goodbye
To linen and silk.
Hello to fabrics that hold their own
With regurgitated milk.

How to protect one's clothing,
Is something of a riddle;
No matter what, you'll be adorned
By Babe's own-label dribble.

Whenever Baby does a burp
One fact you'll have to face,
No matter where that muslin is
IT WON'T BE THE RIGHT PLACE.

So please do take this sound advice
And try to fill that closet
Exclusively with garments
That will tone just right with posset!

Judy Rose

On Platform 5

I watch you gripping your hands
that have grown into the familiar contours
of old age, waiting for the train
to begin its terrifying journey
back to yourself, to your small house
where the daily habit of being alone
will have to be learnt all over again.

Whatever you do with your lined face
nothing disguises that look in your eyes.
Between you and your family
words push like passengers until
your daughter kisses you goodbye –
uttering those parting platitudes
that spill about the closing of a door.

For them your visit's over and relief
jerks in the hands half-lifted now to wave.
Soon there will be far distances between
and duty letters counting out your year.
A whistle blows. The station moves away.
A magazine stays clenched upon your lap.
And your white knuckles tighten round each fear.

Edward Storey

When I was a Child

For my mother I run to the slipway
herring gulls pick around boats
shake spread wings, lift away, heckling
sand gleams to the water's brown edge
I'm shy of the bustle round nets
the loud men's voices
I run home, hugging damp papers.
Inside them, fish gasp.

In the kitchen the papers sprawl open
the fish pump, thrusting and gape-mouthed
they dim just as we watch them.

Under a cold sluice of water
she severs the slippery head
the flat eyes stare up at me
I fan out the tails as she tosses them
and watch her, finger-crooked
squeeze out the squirt of the entrails
bubbled on their clot of dark blood
she firms the fish with her palm

and slices it, eases
flesh over spine
I peel off the delicate comb of its bones
ruffle red water with it.

'When I was a child,' she says
'I stretched skins for my father to cobble.'
'Did they feel like cows?'
I'd never seen cows
their slop mouths
the swell of their bellies
heard the strain of their voices in dark barns
smelt the milk-sweetness of them
been timid, yet, at the swaying bulk of their sides.

'They felt colder than cows,' she said.

Berlie Doherty

65

Two Mangy Cooks

I sat and told my new wife's Dad,
Over a breakfast coffee,
'You might not quite believe me, but
Your daughter can't cook for toffee.

Her scrambled egg's like concrete,
Her bacon tastes like leather,
Her toast! It looks like seaweed
And I'm sure it predicts the weather.'

'Ah! She takes after her mother,
No use to complain or beg,
The first five years are the worst,' he said
As he crunched his second boiled egg.

Ian Larmont

Soup

From the lighted window
I watch my mother
picking leeks in the twilight.

I will have soup
for my supper,
sprinkled with green parsley.

She passes me my creamy bowl.
My hands are warm,
and smell of soap.

My mother's hands are cold as roots.
She shuts up the chickens
by moonlight.

Selima Hill

To Our Daughter

*A*nd she is beautiful, our daughter.
Only six months, but a person.
She turns to look at everything, out walking.
All so precious. I mustn't disturb it with words.
People are like great clowns,
Blossom like balloons, black pigeons like eagles,
Water beyond belief.

She holds out her hand to air,
Sea, sky, wind, sun, movement, stillness,
And wants to hold them all.
My finger is her earth connection, me, and earth.

68

Her head is like an apple, or an egg.
Skin stretched fine over a strong casing,
Her whole being developing from within
And from without: the answer.

And she sings, long notes from the belly or the throat,
Her legs kick her feet up to her nose,
She rests – laid still like a large rose.
She is our child,
The world is not hers, she has to win it.

Jennifer Armitage

Clinic Day

*H*er thin puny little body,
contorted in rage and indignation.
As I placed her in the cold white scoop,
Of the plastic scales.
The self-satisfied clinic mothers,
dangled their fat, round faced,
pink cheeked little monsters.
And gleefully compared notes.
'My little Wayne is taking eight ounces of his feed.'
'He has all his milk teeth has our Arnold.'
'John can count backwards in Urdu.'
I retrieved my scarlet-faced, toothless, wailing banshee.
'How many ounces does she take of her feed?'
enquired Mrs Neat as a new pin.
'I'm not sure, she's breast fed,' I apologised.

A withering look of distaste followed by,
'Oh I always like to see EXACTLY
how much Nigel is taking.'
Exit inferior mother,
with squalling inferior infant.
Social Worker – 'Isn't she walking yet at 15 months?'
'Er no, I'm afraid not.'
'Perhaps if you had all carpet, in the hall and dining room,
she wouldn't be afraid of falling.'
Em tucked one leg under her,
in a sitting position,
and scooted crab-like across the room,
in a defiant gesture, that's my girl!

Jo Barnes

Mother . . . Sister . . . Daughter . . .

'If you should see me,
walking down the street,
mouth muffled
head low against the wind,
know
that this is no woman bent
on sacrifice
just
heavy
with the thoughts
of freedom . . .'

Jean 'Binta' Breeze

Mothers and Daughters

The cruel girls we loved
Are over forty,
Their subtle daughters
Have stolen their beauty;

And with a blue stare
Of cool surprise,
They mock their anxious mothers
With their mothers' eyes.

David Campbell

The Glassy Green and Maroon

Cinderella had glass slippers
I used to believe in because
my mother has always worn
glass bangles of a special kind –
made as I thought from similar glass.

Ma's bangles are thick maroon and dark,
they are green glints and unbreakable
                    I think
because she can wear them all day:
whether she scrubs out clothes
or dishes, the glass bangles stay on.
Afraid of ruining her gold wedding bangles
she somehow trusts the glassy green
and maroon. Every day, broom in hand
she sweeps out the dust
from the verandah, from our doorsteps,
while the glass bangles catch
the morning sun, the afternoon sun . . .

Then finally, when she raises her arms
to undo the scarf protecting her hair,
how the glass bangles glisten, loyal
                    year after year
above her small wrists – bands of lingering light
illuminating her
who would otherwise remain hidden
with her work.

Nowadays I can't find
such sturdy bangles – not in Ahmedabad,
not in Delhi. The glass snaps
like raw spaghetti, like dry twigs
from termite emptied trees,
like rusty barbed wire,
rusty tin shack neighbourhoods
where tin roofs creak against their crookedness
break against the slightest movement
from the wind, from a dog's tail, from a child
                    who walks out the door.

The glass snaps
the bangles break.

Sujata Bhatt

75

Yesterday

It seems only yesterday
I balanced a tiny foot
on my palm
and marvelled
that anything
so perfect
could be so small.
Now I can fit my hand in
when I clean your shoes.

I can remember
when I was centred
round you
feeling your feet
strong and determined
testing the strength
of my rib cage
your hard heels
distorting my belly.

Now I wave you off
in the morning
and turn away
to continue
with my work
unhindered by your
eager face
grateful to be able
to make my own pace.
Yet tuned
to your return.

In time the distance
we put between us
will deprive me
of your grace.
Until then
each simple homely act
like rubbing this polish
into your shoes
will focus
        my imperfect love.

Patricia Pogson

For My Grandmother Knitting

There is no need they say
but the needles still move
their rhythms in the working of your hands
as easily
as if your hands
were once again those sure and skilful hands
of the fisher-girl.

You are old now
and your grasp of things is not so good
but master of your moments then
deft and swift
you slit the still-ticking quick silver fish.
Hard work it was too
of necessity.

But now they say there is no need
as the needles move
in the working of your hands
once the hands of the bride
with the hand-span waist
once the hands of the miner's wife
who scrubbed his back
in a tin bath by the coal fire
once the hands of the mother
of six who made do and mended
scraped and slaved slapped sometimes
when necessary.

But now they say there is no need
the kids they say grandma
have too much already
more than they can wear
too many scarves and cardigans –
gran you do too much
there's no necessity.

At your window you wave
them goodbye Sunday.
With your painful hands
big on shrunken wrists.
Swollen-jointed. Red. Arthritic. Old.
But the needles still move
their rhythms in the working of your hands
easily
as if your hands remembered
of their own accord the pattern
as if your hands had forgotten
how to stop.

Liz Lochhead

Motherless Baby

Motherless baby and babyless mother
Bring them together to love one another.

Christina Rossetti

Human Affection

Mother, I love you so
Said the child, I love you more than I know.
She laid her head on her mother's arm,
And the love between them kept them warm.

Stevie Smith

Broken Moon (for Emma)

Twelve, small as six,
strength, movement, hearing
all given in half measure,
my daughter,
child of genetic carelessness,
walks uphill, always.

I watch her morning face;
precocious patience as she hooks each sock,
creeps it up her foot,
aims her jersey like a quoit.
My fingers twitch;
her private frown deters.

Her jokes can sting:
'My life is like dressed crab
– lot of effort, rather little meat.'
Yet she delights in seedlings taking root,
finding a fossil,
a surprise dessert.

Chopin will not yield to her stiff touch;
I hear her cursing.
She paces Bach exactly,
firm rounding of perfect cadences.
Somewhere inside
she is dancing a courante.

In dreams she skims the sand,
curls toes into the ooze of pools,
leaps on to stanchions.
Awake, her cousins take her hands;
they lean into the waves,
stick-child between curved sturdiness.

She turns away from stares,
laughs at the boy who asks
if she will find a midget husband.
Ten years ago, cradling her,
I showed her the slice of silver in the sky.
'Moon broken,' she said.

Carole Satyamurti

83

The Dolls

'Whenever you dress me dolls, mammy,
  Why do you dress them so,
And make them gallant soldiers,
  When never a one I know;
And not as gentle ladies
  With frills and frocks and curls,
As people dress the dollies
  Of other little girls?'

Ah – why did she not answer:–
  'Because your mammy's heed
Is always gallant soldiers,
  As well may be, indeed.
One of them was your daddy,
  His name I must not tell;
He's not the dad who lives here,
  But one I love too well.'

Thomas Hardy

Uniform

'You'll grow,' she said and that was that. No use
To argue and to sulk invited slaps.
The empty shoulders drooped, the sleeves hung loose –
No use – she nods and the assistant wraps.

New blazer, new school socks and all between
Designed for pea pod anonymity.
All underwear the regulation green;
Alike there's none to envy, none to pity.

At home she feasts on pins. She tacks and tucks
Takes in the generous seams and smiles at thrift.
I fidget as she fits. She tuts and clucks.
With each neat stitch she digs a deeper rift.

They'll mock me with her turnings and her hem
And laugh and know that I'm not one of them.

Jan Dean

85

Whose Baby?

The spoon misses her mouth
She bangs it on the table in frustration.
She likes to feed herself
And cries if I help her.

I bring her a mirror
I wipe the food off her face.
She watches her life
Going backwards.

She can't walk or crawl
But has already passed her exams,
Been married and read more books
Than I ever could.

Now I read to her at night
And I struggle with words
Which are easy for her mind
But impossible on her lips.

'Good night, Mum,' I whisper.
The crooked smile she returns
Is not at all like a baby's
Though it still says everything she can't.

Lindsay MacRae

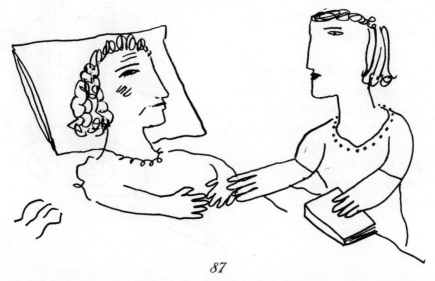

Science, 1953

It was called Domestic Science then.
Formica no more heard of than moon travel,
Beatles, tights or Home Econ.,
each wooden table must be scrubbed
(scrubbed hard and long)
after each shapeless pasty,
limp cucumber sandwich,
had earned its sad D+
from school, and later home.
To me they tasted fine.

Miss explained that only *tops*
of frying pans required a shine,
as blackened bottoms drew more heat.
Highly scientific, so we thought,
but not my mother.
Slapdash and dirty, she's a fool,
my mother muttered, crossly
brandishing wire wool.

She was not noted for her scientific flair;
I less still for my domestic skill.
Yet three domesticated decades on
I live with blackened proof
that science won.

Judith Nicholls

Praise Song for My Mother

You were
water to me
deep and bold and fathoming

You were
moon's eye to me
pull and grained and mantling

You were
sunrise to me
rise and warm and streaming

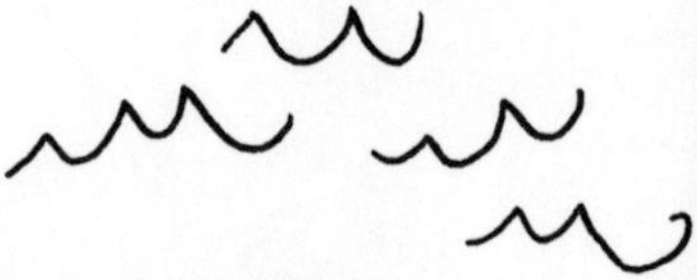

You were
the fishes red gill to me
the flame tree's spread to me
the crab's leg/the fried plantain smell
                    replenishing replenishing
Go to your wide futures, you said

Grace Nichols

Two Old Women

The two of us sit in the doorway,
chatting about our children and grandchildren.
We sink happily
into our oldwomanhood.

Like two spoons
sinking
into a bowl of hot porridge.

Anna Swir

It's Mother, You See

*I*t's mother, you see.

I cannot fold her up like a pram or a bicycle.
It's every day crawling around the agencies.
I cannot leave her alone in a furnished room.
She has to come with me, arm in arm, umbrella'd,
Or trailing a little.

She is thin in wind and limb,
She is not quite white in the head,
Now and then she stops – suddenly and completely
Like a mutinous dog on a lead.

(And once, long ago, in reverse,
I trailed after *her* skirts in the throng street,
Her basket of goodies
Bobbing just out of my reach)

She's no need to stare at the shops.
We have plenty more clothes, if we bothered to open the cases,
And hundreds of photographs of the way things were.
Sometimes we take out a bit of the better china
And wash it and put it away again.

It is every day to the agents,
Then on to the library, checking the papers for ads.
Or walking the streets, looking for signs that might say
Where to apply for a key.

It is hard on the legs, it is hard on the wits and the heart,
But I cannot leave her alone in a furnished room.
O come *on*, Mum. One day we'll find us a home
Somewhere this side of the sky.

Elma Mitchell

Tell Me, Tell Me, Sarah Jane

Tell me, tell me, Sarah Jane,
  Tell me, dearest daughter,
Why are you holding in your hand
  A thimbleful of water?
Why do you hold it to your eye
  And gaze both late and soon
From early morning light until
  The rising of the moon?

Mother, I hear the mermaids cry,
  I hear the mermen sing,
And I can see the sailing-ships
  All made of sticks and string.
And I can see the jumping fish,
  The whales that fall and rise
And swim about the waterspout
  That swarms up to the skies.

Tell me, tell me, Sarah Jane,
  Tell your darling mother,
Why do you walk beside the tide

94

As though you loved none other?
Why do you listen to a shell
  And watch the billows curl,
And throw away your diamond ring
  And wear instead the pearl?

Mother I hear the water
  Beneath the headland pinned,
And I can see the sea-gull
  Sliding down the wind.
I taste the salt upon my tongue
  As sweet as sweet can be.

Tell me, my dear, whose voice you hear?

It is the sea, the sea.

Charles Causley

Acknowledgements

The publishers gratefully acknowledge the following permission to reproduce copyright material in this book.

The poem reprinted on page 9 is from *No Holds Barred* The Raving Beauties Choose New Poems by Women, published in Great Britain by The Women's Press Ltd, 1985, 34 Great Sutton Street, London EC1V 0LQ; 'Lemon Sole' © Helen Dunmore, from *Secrets* published by Bodley Head. Reprinted by permission of AP Watt Ltd; 'Woman Enough' Copyright © 1979, 1991, Erica Mann Jong, all rights reserved. Used by permission of the poet; 'Folding Sheets (copyright © 1985 by Middlemarsh, Inc.) from *My Mother's Body* Alfred A Knopf, Inc. New York. Reprinted by permission of A M Heath & Co. Ltd; 'My Mother' by Medbh McGuchian from *The Flower Master and Other Poems*, published by The Gallery Press (1993). Reprinted by kind permission of the author and The Gallery Press; 'Eat Your Veg' copyright © Valerie Bloom 2000 from *The World is Sweet* published by Bloomsbury; 'Fanfare' copyright © UA Fanthorpe from *Standing To* (1982). Reproduced by permission of Peterloo Poets; 'The Moment' from *The Dead and the Living* by Sharon Olds. Copyright © 1983 by Sharon Olds. Reprinted by permission of Alfred A Knopf, a division of Random House Inc; 'Small Incident in a Library' copyright © David Sutton from *Flints* (1986). Reproduced by permission of Peterloo Poets; 'Morning Song' from *Collected Poems* by Sylvia Plath published by Faber and Faber Ltd. Reprinted by permission of Faber and Faber Ltd; 'Lullaby' © 1990 Rosemary Norman, reprinted by permission of the author. First printed in *In the Gold of Flesh* (1990) by the Women's Press, later featured in *I Wouldn't Thank You For a Valentine*, published by Viking; 'Poem for a Daughter' copyright © Anne Stevenson and Bloodaxe Books. Reprinted by permission of the author; 'Young' by Anne Sexton, reprinted by permission of Sterling Lord Literistic, Inc. Copyright Anne Sexton; 'Annie (1868-1944)' by Gillian Clarke from *Letting in the Rumour* published by Carcanet Press Limited. Reprinted by Permission of Carcanet Press Limited; 'Names' from *Serious Concerns* by Wendy Cope published by Faber and Faber Ltd. Reprinted by permission of Faber and Faber Ltd; 'A Frosty Night' by Robert Graves from *Complete Poems* published by Carcanet Press Limited. Reprinted by permission of Carcanet Press Limited; 'Gift for Rebecca' © Isobel Thrilling. Reprinted by permission of Isobel Thrilling; By kind permission of Judy Rose c/o Caroline Sheldon Literary Agency: 'Dressed to Spill' from *Mummy Said the "B" Word* published by Headline 1997; 'On Platform 5' © Edward Storey. Reprinted by permission of Edward Storey; Ian Larmont: 'Two Mangy Cooks' © 2000 Ian Larmont; The poem reprinted on page 67 is from *No Holds Barred* The Raving Beauties Choose New Poems by Women, published in Great Britain by The Women's Press Ltd, 1985, 34 Great Sutton Street, London EC1V 0LQ; 'Mother Sister Daughter' from the Virago Press book *Spring Cleaning* by Jean Binta Breeze, published by permission of Little Brown; 'The Glassy Green and Maroon' by Sujata Bhatt from *Monkey Shadows* published by Carcanet Press Limited. Reprinted by permission of Carcanet Press Limited; 'Yesterday' © Patricia Pogson. Reprinted by permission of Patricia Pogson; 'For My Grandmother Knitting', from *Dreaming Frankenstein* by Liz Lochhead published by Polygon. Reprinted by permission of Polygon; 'Human Affection' by Stevie Smith published by permission of The Stevie Smith Estate; 'Broken Moon' from *Selected Poems* by Carole Satyamurti published by Bloodaxe Books 1998. Reprinted by permission of the author; 'Whose Baby' (p.41, 20 lines) from *You Canny Shove Yer Granny off a Bus!* By Lindsay MacRae (Viking 1995). Copyright © Lindsay MacRae, 1995; 'Science, 1953' © Judith Nicholls 1994 from *Storm's Eye* by Judith Nicholls, published by Oxford University Press. Reprinted by permission of the author; 'Praise Song for My Mother' by Grace Nichols from *Fat Black Woman's Poems* published by Virago Press. Reprinted by permission of Little Brown and Company (UK); The poem reprinted on page 91 is from *No Holds Barred* The Raving Beauties Choose New Poems by Women, published in Great Britain by The Women's Press Ltd, 1985, 34 Great Sutton Street, London EC1V 0LQ; 'It's Mother, You See' copyright © Elma Mitchell from *Furnished Rooms*. Reproduced by permission of Peterloo Poets; 'Tell Me, Tell Me, Sarah Jane' by Charles Causley from *The Poems* published by Macmillan. Reprinted by permission of David Higham Associates.

Every effort has been made to trace the copyright holders. The publishers would like to hear from any copyright holder not acknowledged.